Soul Catcher Episode 1

Accidental Ghost

Elle Klass

Soul Catcher Episode 1

Copyright©2023 by Elle Klass
Published by Books by Elle, Inc.
ISBN: 978-1-951017-38-5

Editor Dawn Lewis

Author's Disclaimer

Soul Catcher Episode 1

Books in the Realm Walker Series
In the Shadows
The Land of Lost Souls
Hidden Passages
The Ring of Betrayal

Other Realm Walker Companion Books
The Origin: Marya's Journal

Realm Walker World Books – coming soon!
Love at Frost Bite
Accidental Ghost: Soul Catcher Episode.1

Other Young Adults Series
The Bloodseeker
Zombie Girl
Hidden Journals
Baby Girl

Once Upon Academy Shorts
Bone Stars

For other shorts and stories find Elle Klass as Elle Klass on Patreon.

1

Halloween came every day for me since I fell into a river of blood in a realm I'd never heard of. It was innocent. I was spelunking when I dropped through a cavern and into Blood River. Terra, an elf hybrid, saved me. She even got me back home after I was kidnapped by vampires and escaped to Thraves, land of the harvesters, where I met death and learned my destiny. Sometimes I'd give my soul to return to my former life.

Soul Catcher Episode 1

I dropped the pickaxe. I wouldn't get the hang of it. The pick wasn't working for me.

I glanced at my trainer in his spirit form.

"I'll never get it right."

"You will."

"I'm your punishment, aren't I?" He was a prominent tribunal diplomat for the Harvester realm of Thraves before I dropped into his realm while spelunking.

"No. My punishment is being kicked off the tribunal because of my own actions."

There were eight realms, all of them represented on the tribunal except the human realm or Lols (Land of Lost Souls). They called us commoners. We were anything but common and I resented being called common.

"We'll try again tomorrow."

"Sure." I climbed the steps to the brownstone. He vanished into the night, his spirit returning to Thraves. Harvesters could only harvest souls in Lols in spirit form. I had a beef with this realm being called that. Souls here weren't lost, we were home on Earth, or wherever it was. As a harvester hybrid, I could harvest in my physical form.

I rolled the rocks from each realm between my fingers. I was a hybrid of five realms - Verboten, Aradia, Sier, Canida, and Thraves - meaning I was a troll, elf, dragon, Lycan, and harvester hybrid. According to death, I not only had to collect a rock from each realm but had to enter it, which I had. I didn't know what good the Drakonian rock did since I wasn't vampire, but death insisted it was useful. She was cryptic.

I bore the mark of each realm on my chest. A passport that allowed me to enter and exit any realm I was part of.

Harvesting wasn't a perfect science and Metford, my instructor, and I were learning together. Evidently, harvester hybrids weren't common.

That was six months ago. I had improved in the art of harvesting but still had some troubles.

The dark soul latched onto my pickaxe and wouldn't let go. I hit the end on the ground, hoping to jar it loose, but it clung like sticky goo.

"Easy. Don't let frustration get you."

Soul Catcher Episode 1

Easy for him to say. Metford was born in Thraves and designed for harvesting. I held the pickaxe upward like he'd taught me. The black ball rose finally. It was ascending to the Otherworld. The place dark souls go.

No, no, no, I screamed in my head as a tiny piece of it stuck. It looked like a black blob of stretched slime. The yellow stone in the eye of the pickaxe flashed.

One of the rocks used to trap the souls was blinking in and out. When a soul was trapped, they shone bright, connecting in a six-point star. I kept the pickaxe steady as I maneuvered myself to the rock then carefully lowered myself.

I kept the pickaxe as stable as I could with one hand, lowered myself and touched the rock. Its energy returned and the pesky dark soul continued its ascension as the tiny stuck piece became unstuck.

I dropped the axe and sighed.

"You're improving," Metford said in a congratulatory tone.

I held up my hand to high five but his spirit hand went right through mine.

2

My eyelids drooped even as I worked to keep them open. Taking another gulp of my double shot iced coffee wasn't enough. Harvesting and early morning classes didn't work, but it was the only time this class was offered.

Dr. Blyzbub took her glasses off, twirling them in her hand as she spoke. "Vickery House in upstate New York is an example of spirit attachment to a structure. Several families moved in and were scared out after complaints of paranormal events. The families all lived ghost-free lives after leaving. It has been said the house could be a gateway between the living and the dead. The house has been unoccupied since 1947."

Thanks to being a harvester, I now had a double major; paranormal studies and geology, which meant sleepless nights for the next three years. Adding paranormal studies meant more classes. Therefore, I take a class at eight in the morning instead of sleeping. Dr. Blyzbub was full of stories of hauntings. This weekend I'd check out Vickery House.

I searched it on my laptop and saved the address. It was in the town of Blake. A small, quintessential town with cobblestone streets and mom and pop locally owned shops.

Vickery House put it on the map. They don't do tours in the house but it is part of a tour of Blake.

I stuffed my laptop into my bag and pulled it over my shoulder. It was time to go home and sleep before tonight's harvesting.

"How about a coffee?" Sharae asked.

She was hot, sweet, and had been flirting with me since the beginning of the semester, but I didn't have time to date and I had a thing for a girl I hadn't seen in months – Terra.

Soul Catcher Episode 1

The girl who saved me in Drakonia. What we had was an attraction and it hadn't gone beyond a couple kisses, but I couldn't get her out of my mind.

Our destinies weren't intertwined. I was stuck here harvesting and she was saving the realms.

It was time to move on, but not today. My bed was calling. "Thanks, but not today. I had a late night." Her face dropped as the words left my mouth. I'd turned her down so many times.

Her deep brown eyes turned downward. "Sure, another time."

I felt like roadkill driven over by many cars.

I liked her. What wasn't to like? She had the right size curves, a sweet smile, a caramel complexion, endless brown eyes, and was interested in the dead.

My alarm went off, its annoying ring blasting in my ear. I chose it so I'd wake up. Rings that weren't obnoxious became part of my dreams and I slept through them.

I slid the ringer off instead of hitting snooze and got up, my stomach complaining about being empty. A side-effect of being a

Soul Catcher Episode 1

full-time student with a double major and moonlighting as a harvester was never having time to shop or do laundry. I pulled on a pair of sweats that smelled freshish and slipped on a pair of shoes.

The beauty of living in New York was food was always close.

I picked up all the clothes on my floor and tossed them into a bag with soap pods and dryer sheets. There was a laundromat on the corner before the coffee shop.

After tossing my clothes in the machine I walked next door and ordered a ham and cheese croissant and double shot iced coffee.

I turned on my computer and continued my research of Vickery House.

It seemed a pretty typical haunting, an unrested dark soul. Noises like scraping against the floor and even in the heat of the summer a specific room was chilly.

Wait, maybe not so typical. A young couple bought the house in the spring of 1946. His niece came to live with them after her mother died. Soon, she started talking to herself, carrying on conversations that escalated into her sleepwalking and eventually the girl refused to go back into the house. She interacted with the spirit. Maybe she was a harvester hybrid, too. She went home to her father but the nonsense didn't stop and eventually she killed herself.

Spirits of unrest generally went about their business the day they died, repeating it day after day. This one hadn't.

No one ever died in the house, but its occupants always complained of the same things; strange noises and a freezing room. Of course, anyone who ever lived in the house was dead and no one ever died in the house.

I finished my clothes, returned to my brownstone and showered.

Metford's voice entered my head from the comicay, a gel device that fit above the wrist. The harvesters gave it to me. It was used for communication among other things.

Our meeting place tonight was the Candy Mill in Vanguard, Pennsylvania.

The elevators or gateways made it much easier to travel the land of the living and get there quickly. They were a static disturbance, found often times in cemeteries but not always. As a harvester who saw spirits, the ones in cemeteries were the easiest for me to find. They allowed me travel anywhere in

Lols. I stepped in and thought of where I was going. The elevator vanished as I stood on the sidewalk outside the candy store.

Did someone fall into a vat of chocolate and drown or eat too much taffy?

Metford appeared at my side. He was tall and thick with a goatee he was always tugging at when I was in the middle of harvesting. It was a nervous habit, and lately he didn't tug so much. I was getting better.

"A honeymooning couple died in the hotel across the street in 1993. It was a double homicide, and the killer was never apprehended."

I never asked where he got his info. My eyes swept the hotel. It was several stories high.

"It was in room 513."

Great. Metford stayed at my side, filling me in on the details of the couple's death as I strolled into the hotel.

Situated on the left was a large, circular check-in counter. To the right were plush, sage-colored couches and chairs, and wooden tables. A large mural of a river and woods in a modern style was painted on one wall.

Soul Catcher Episode 1

The clerk at the counter smiled as I walked past him as if I was a guest returning from dinner. No one but me could see Metford, as he was in spirit form. Sometimes I forgot and talked back to him. I got strange looks when that happened.

I pressed the button and waited as the elevator ascended and the doors opened.

I didn't really have a plan but was hoping the room would be empty.

I knocked on 513 and didn't get an answer. That was good. I slid the stone from Sier over the card pad and the door unlocked. Each stone did its own special thing.

Once inside, I dropped my harvester bag onto the bed. It was a designer bag I found at the secondhand shop. I guessed its previous owner got rid of it for the next year's style. It worked. I looked inconspicuous and the pickaxe fit into it nicely without catching any eyes.

I placed the rocks at equal points in the middle of the room after rubbing them together in my hands. The process recharged them. I grabbed the pickaxe and waited.

Soul Catcher Episode 1

The couple had returned about nine according to the night clerk. Their screams were heard about an hour later. It was 8:56.

At 9:07, the couple came in kissing, their hands all over each other. Clothes dropped to the floor and I turned. They were dead, but it still felt like an invasion of their privacy. Not really a horrible thing to make love before dying. I'd seen worse in my six months of harvesting.

I let the rocks do their thing as the couple's spirits coalesced into the center of them.

I touched the female as she was closest, her soul shining white on the pick. I brought it upward and watched as her spirit ascended. I then touched the man's soul, also white, both pure souls, and raised the pick.

The door opened. Fudge! I looked to Metford like he could help but, as a spirit, there was nothing he could do.

The man's spirit ascended. It would have been an easy job. Pure souls usually were.

A tall man stared at me, his mouth gaping. I guessed he'd never seen a 19-year-old with a pickaxe in a hotel. He looked like a businessman with his expensive suit, short, combed back, wavy hair, and clean-shaven face. By his unsteady gait it appeared he'd had a few too many drinks as he stumbled towards me and fell.

I tried to slip out of the way but couldn't in time as his shoulder dropped onto my arm that held the pickaxe.

In a panic, I flipped him over with my free hand and sighed relief when it had only grazed him. Dribbles of blood bubbled around the wound.

"Leave him," Metford said, tugging his goatee so hard I thought he'd pull it out.

"I can't. He's hurt."

"You're here to harvest souls. He'll heal from the injury."

Sure he would, but I couldn't leave him like that. I ran to the bathroom and wet a washcloth and pressed it against his arm until the bleeding stopped.

Metford grumbled something as I rummaged around the man's cosmetic bag in search of bandages.

At the bottom of the bag, and looking as if they'd been in the bag for years, the wrappers discolored and wrinkled, were two regular size adhesive bandages. I ripped the wrappers off and pressed them over the wound.

"Since you interfered and shouldn't have, don't leave anything at the scene," Metford scolded.

I wore gloves, always. They were part of my kit. I lashed back at him, "What if he had died? How can you be so cold?"

I collected the rocks and put them back into the velvet bag I kept them in, then the pickaxe and, last, I rolled up the bloody washcloth and tossed it in the bag.

"I'm not uncaring," Metford claimed as if trying to convince himself.

"What would I have done if he'd died besides harvest his soul?"

"That didn't happen."

"But what if it had?" I imagined myself with a murder rap. I'd be guilty with no excuse. I was sure harvesting souls wouldn't count as an excuse for an accidental murder. I'd be laughed out of court and sentenced, or I'd have to plea.

3

As if I didn't have sleeping problems already, I kept reliving the moment the man landed on the pick end of my pickaxe every time I closed my eyes, the scrape of it brushing his skin sounding in my ears.

Dr. Blyzbub didn't have everything right but she did have good ghost stories. When Saturday rolled around, I packed my gear and went to Blake, NY.

I'd booked a tour and, as the website said, it went past Vickery House and the cemetery. As a harvester hybrid it was important to know where I could find a gateway and most cemeteries had them.

The home was over two centuries old, built in 1760, just before the American Revolution. The landscaping had been maintained but nobody had stepped foot in the house since 1947 when the young couple moved out, according to the guide.

It was a colonial-style home. The blue paint kept up and many vines trimmed down. The second window on the left side of the second floor is where all the complaints from owners came from. The guide suggested if you watched closely you might see a ghost of Vickery House, named after its first owner who died in his late 90s in 1801. He lived alone in that big house. His name Samual Vickery.

I didn't see a thing from the street, but the window had the least amount of vines and blockages surrounding it, as if they wanted people to focus on that window. They gave us EMF meters and let us roam the grounds.

A high fence surrounded the acreage. I guessed it was all for money. Without trying to look too obvious, I scanned the fence for a way to enter besides the obvious front gate. I found one with vines tossed over it. I figured they didn't want people breaking in and searching the grounds with their own devices.

"Found anything yet?" asked a kid, about sixteen, wearing a red ball cap. He had clumps of dark freckles under his brown eyes.

"No," I said in disappointment. I wasn't, but it added to my act of being a tourist.

"I think it's a scam. These little towns all have haunted houses," he said, as if he was an expert.

"You've been to others?"

"Yeah, my dad is a ghost hunter. He gets paid to find ghosts. We never really do find any ghosts, but he gets good publicity, and he makes a good living."

I noted the skepticism in his voice. "You don't believe in ghosts, do you?"

"Nah. I mean the closest thing I ever saw was a chair that rocked on its own. It wasn't caused by a ghost but an uneven floor."

Well, well, a nonbeliever. I won't be the one to school him on the reality of ghosts. The less attention I got, the better.

Soul Catcher Episode 1

He pulled a phone from his back pocket. "My dad. Have fun. Don't watch that meter too closely."

I wouldn't. If there were spirits, I'd see them. The meter was to fit in and the tour was to learn.

After the tour, I grabbed lunch. The kid and his dad walked into the cafe. I recognized the kid's ball cap but didn't pay more attention until they walked past me. The kid smiled and the fathers' eyes met mine. His hair tussled and the expensive suit absent. I recognized him as the man from the hotel. *What were the odds?*

A ghost hunter staying in a hotel room where two people were murdered. Of course. Too bad I cleared out the ghosts for him. I'd do the same here if there were ghosts, only I'd be ending their souls' torment.

I needed to know what their plan was, no more incidents. I finished my lunch, attempting to listen in on their conversation but with all the chatter in the cafe it was difficult to pinpoint.

They sat a couple booths down from mine, the kid with his back to me. His father, the ghost hunter, glanced at me with a glint of recognition. It was like he was trying to place where he'd seen me. I doubted he remembered anything as he was too drunk that night in the hotel.

My glance drifted to the bandage on his arm. I couldn't help but feel a little guilty. Correction: a lot guilty. That's why I'd been having dreams of that night.

"I didn't get any readings," I said, approaching the table. Chatting with them was an exploratory mission.

The kid turned around. "No shame. You probably never will."

The father narrowed his eyes. "William's a skeptic but I like to keep an open mind. Mike," he held out a hand.

"Ghost hunter extraordinaire," the son followed up with, rolling his eyes.

"A ghost hunter. I think that's fascinating," I said. "I'm a paranormal studies major."

Mike's eyes lit up as if he had a token ear to tell ghostly tales of his scam career. "Join us. I have a story or two I can share."

He wasn't humble. "Thanks, are you sure? I don't want to interrupt," I said coyly.

"Never," Mike insisted.

Soul Catcher Episode 1

The son rolled his eyes. I guessed he was used to the spiel.

He went into a couple stories that should have sent shivers up my spine, except I saw actual ghosts and the worst part was figuring out how to harvest their souls.

"What about Vickery House?"

"I think it's a bust, but that's why I'm here. I get paid to look for ghosts. Thing is, everyone says the place is haunted, even interviewed a couple who claim the bedroom light goes on every night and they see a shadow behind the curtain. No one ever died in that house but Mr. Vickery from natural causes. Maid found him in the morning in bed. He died in his sleep. Best way to go. His bedroom was on the other end of the hall so it's not even his room that's haunted..." He paused. "I think a small town like this needs a good ghost story."

"Yeah," I agreed. "You going there tonight?"

He glanced at his watch. "We're going to get some rest first. The town commissioner is meeting us tonight about ten with the keys. You can join if you want, always needing an extra hand."

20

"Thanks, but I'm going to have to sit this one out. My mom is expecting me later tonight. This was a stop on my way home for the weekend."

"Like your tat," the son said, staring at my arm.

I had a snake chasing its tail on my bicep. "Thanks. It means rebirth."

The son nodded. "Sweet!"

I hadn't thought much about how cliché it was that I, a harvester, had a tattoo meaning rebirth or the cycle of life and death. I'd had it for a couple years before I knew what I was. I guess a part of me always knew.

Mike handed me a card. I thanked him and left.

I had plenty of time to get to Vickery House, do what I do, and leave. I glanced at the card: Mike Medallion, Ghost Hunter. *Was Medallion really his name?* I doubted it.

I couldn't believe people actually paid for this stuff.

I went to the back gate, lifted the heavy vines that were used to hide it and, to my surprise, it was unlocked. The property was surrounded by trees on three sides. This didn't speak volumes for actual ghosts but had scam written all over it. They left the gate unlocked for whatever seedy person they paid to enter the house, flip on the lights and stand in front of the window.

I pressed the Troll key against the door lock. It molded itself into a key and the lock clicked when I turned. Verboten was filled with gems and metals and trolls were famous as smiths. I guessed that's why the rock worked to mold a temp key. Once I pulled it off the lock it went back to its natural form.

The old door creaked open, sunlight bathing a large kitchen. I ran my gloved finger along the kitchen counter. No dust, like the place had been cleaned recently. So much for no one being in the house since 1947.

In the formal dining room was a long wooden table with eight chairs. The living room, or parlor or whatever it was called, was open with an absent ceiling. Gleaming wood flooring caught the sun's light.

The staircase was off the foyer. My eyes followed it. Three rooms on one side and three on the other. The wooden banister made an oval until it ended at a wall. The rooms were all open, spreading light in the living room and foyer. It was time to get to work. No dust on the banister either, I noted as I walked up the steps.

Maybe they cleaned it because doofus scammer Mike the ghost hunter would be doing a gig there. I was sure having him there filming fake evidence of ghosts would be helpful and fill the town coffers with more money.

An authentically dusty house would be spookier. The second bedroom was wallpapered in a white print with raised paisley. It was actual fabric and soft. The curtain wide open, the window gave a praiseworthy view of the town.

Sheer white fabric fell over the sides of the metal canopy over the bed. A large mirror adorned the door of the wardrobe. I didn't touch anything, remembering what Metford always told me. My job wasn't to disturb, but to save souls.

I placed the rocks around the room in the six-point fashion. Sier, the realm of dragons always at the top, and worked them around clockwise. I waited. If there were spirits in the room the rocks would draw them out and suck them in.

A car door slamming woke me up. *When had I fallen asleep?* That was sloppy. Now I had to get out before Mike and the kid entered and caught me. I glanced at the rocks. Nothing. The center was empty. No ghosts. I wasn't shocked. I collected the rocks and stuffed them into my bag and headed downstairs, but turned around when the front door opened as the steps led directly to the foyer.

Three voices drifted up the stairs as I hid behind a wall to the right. I recognized Mike and the kid, William, but not the other. I guessed that was the city commissioner who let them in.

Stay calm and think. There was a closed door to my right. I twisted the knob but it was locked. *Of all the things!* Digging into my gear I found the velvet bag containing the rocks and poured them into my palm.

Footfalls sounded on the steps and from below I heard Mike say, "Put everything there and we'll get it set up."

I sank into the shadowy corner near the door to be as invisible as possible and held my breath as the footfalls stopped at the top of the stairs. *Go left, go left,* I repeated in my mind.

The footfalls started again as they moved towards the other end. I let out my breath slowly and dumped the stones into my palm. One hit the floor and the footfalls stopped. I imagined Mike pausing and glancing my way.

When the steps started up again, clearly heading away from me, I leaned down and collected the stone. I dropped all of them back into the bag except the Troll one which I pressed against the lock. It formed a key and unlocked the door.

Soul Catcher Episode 1

I opened the door slowly so as not to alert Mike and slipped inside the room. It was huge and an ugly contrast to the bright airy room I fell asleep in. Antlers hung over a solid, chunky wood bed. The pillars on the bed were thicker than my waist. It looked like something a giant or barbarian slept in.

Starlight through the open window shone on the deep red walls. It could win an award for testosterone ugly rooms.

I might have been curious why the room was locked if it hadn't become extremely clear. A figure moved from the shadows to the right of the bed. It stopped in the middle of the room, turned its head, and stared directly at me with eyes like fire.

I swallowed hard and goosepimples ran up my spine. Ghosts never saw me, how did this one? It moved towards me and I backed towards the wall. *My rocks!* The velvet bag was still in my hand. I dumped them and hurriedly placed them in the locations, hoping to suck it in and trap it

I wasn't quick enough, as the spirit walked through me to the door. *It didn't see me, or did it?* It looked right at me. I spun around as it neared the door. It was looking at something else. My curiosity wanted to know but I hadn't forgotten Mike and the boy. I stifled my curious nature and focused on the spirit. Putting the last stone in place, I stepped out and moved towards the center of the room.

The spirit elongated as the rocks drew it in. It bounced inside the circle as it fought, coalescing into a dark ball. Its mouth opened as it screeched in a high-pitched tone that felt like a knife going through my skull. I dropped to my knees in agony.

I needed my pickaxe, but I'd dropped my bag by the door. Sloppy. I needed to be more mindful but his fiery eyes distracted me. On hands and knees, my head feeling like something was stabbing it repeatedly, I crawled towards it. Reaching the bag, I dug my hand in and pulled out my pickaxe. The spirit pulled towards me then and into the circle. It bounced back as it couldn't break the circle created by the rocks. It screeched again as it flew towards the barrier in anger. The fire in its eyes like rising flames.

I pulled myself up and swung the pick into the spirit. With another screech it coalesced into a ball and slid towards the handle like a slug.

No, you don't. I'd never crossed paths with a soul like this. The pure souls were easy. They didn't fight their ascension to Tranquility but the dark souls hated to let go. They feared the Otherworld but this one was strong and defiant and heavy. As I lifted the pickaxe upwards towards the center of the circle it pushed against me.

You mean, black, stubborn glob! Both hands tight around the wooden handle, I fought its power and lifted upwards. The soul stretched from the pick, screeching horribly as if in pain. It stretched more and more, doing its best to stay there. Little by little, more and more of it ascended.

"What the…"

I glanced in the direction of the voice. Mike stood in the doorway, mouth agape and eyes wide. I met his gaze and recognition hit him. He remembered me. "The… the… you…" he said, unable to form his words as he stumbled backwards and hit the banister before tripping on the first step.

He vanished from my sight as he fell down the steps. I cringed as his body

plummeted down the stairs, causing loud thumping against the wooden steps and the crunching of what sounded like multiple bones crashing to the first floor.
Oh no!

5

My instinct was to rush down the stairs but the pickaxe in my hand refocused my attention. I'd lowered it, lost my focus on harvesting the dark soul and now it was gone. Had it finally given up and moved to the Otherworld or had it gotten away and hidden somewhere in the shadows?

I really messed things up. A man might be dead because of me and, if so, his soul wouldn't be harvested. He wouldn't be on the list. It was accidental because of my meddling. I was in deep trouble with the harvesters if they found out about this. I slung my pickaxe into my designer bag and collected the stones. 'Dad, Dad,' a teary voice filled my ears.

Staying against the wall, I peeked my head out far enough to see down the stairs. William was slumped over his father, calling as if he was trying to wake him from a hard sleep. One of Mike's legs bent in an unnatural fashion.

My conscience battled with itself. I had to get out, but my humanity encouraged me to run down the stairs. *No, no, no.* The first harvester rule was to not get involved, to hang back, do my job and get out. I didn't even know if I did my job. The dark soul could be lingering behind me.

The boy stood then ran away towards another room, possibly to get a phone. He'd be back soon so it was now or never. I slipped down the steps and turned the corner into the kitchen, exiting the way I came.

They'd invited me. I could turn back, pretend to take them up on their offer. *No, no, I couldn't.* If I did, that could mean questioning by the police. My guilt wouldn't keep it together.

Where was the cemetery? I knew where I was, but trees surrounded me on all sides.

Soul Catcher Episode 1

Where were ghosts when I needed one? They were my ticket to finding the cemetery and elevator home. I stopped running and caught my breath. A siren wailed in the distance.

He'd called an ambulance. *Get it together, Tania.* Ghosts like cemeteries. On the tour we stopped at one, but in which direction did I need to go? I pulled the phone out of my jeans pocket and did a search. Collecting myself, I followed the digital voice to the road, flipped my hood over my head and stuffed my hands in the pockets of my jacket.

The house behind me, I didn't glance back. *Had William seen me?* A police car rolled towards me. I stepped behind a thick tree. *No, he was in another room when I slipped out of the house.* The police car swept past me. No one was looking for me.

I turned on the next street, feeling better the more distance I put between myself and the house. Metford would ring me a new one. I did exactly what he always told me not to, but I was doing my job harvesting souls.

It went horribly wrong, but wasn't my fault. I'd fallen asleep waiting for spirits that never arrived because the one haunting the house was a strong, dark spirit that may have

32

gotten away. Didn't Mike say the original owner, Samual Vickery, was the only person to die in the house? Yes, he did, and of natural causes. He was an old man.

A cemetery was like a bug zapper to ghosts. The closer I got the more I crossed paths with them. I didn't have time to harvest these poor souls tonight. I needed to get out of town. The disturbance in the atmosphere noticeable by the shift in my vision. Elevators were almost always near cemeteries but could be found other places to.

My heart skipped a beat as I ran towards it. I'd come back and finish what I started, I thought as I stepped into the elevator then cleared my mind and envisioned my studio apartment.

6

At the last minute my parents' home flashed in my mind, pushing out thoughts of my studio. When the elevator vanished I was standing in the driveway of my parents' home, moonlight shining against my mother's dark blue car in the driveway. *Shit!*

My brain, so frazzled and horrified, it did what it did and thought of safety – my parents. The closest cemetery was miles away and not something I wanted to walk in during the dead of a chilly night. Reluctantly, I headed up the driveway and followed the cement path with seasonal blue and violet flowers on either side to the front door.

I pulled out my key and stuck it in the lock then slid the door open. My mom in a worn purple bath robe stared at me with wide eyes as if I was an intruder. "It's been a while and I uh…missed you," I said in the cheekiest of voices with an unflattering painted smile. She'd read right through me.

"I'm just surprised to see you at two in the morning," my mom said in her *what the hell* voice.

I lowered my smile. "I'll be going to my room." I stepped away from her.

"No, umm…" she stumbled over her words, "I converted your room to an office for work."

Already? I'd only been gone three semesters and they'd gotten rid of my room. I guess they didn't suffer from empty nest syndrome. I couldn't hide the disappointment in my face. "Where is my stuff?"

My mom tilted her head in guilt. "In the guest room but the bed is covered in boxes."

Boxes of my stuff! "I'll take the couch unless it's covered in boxes too," I snapped.

Soul Catcher Episode 1

My mom flopped an arm around my shoulder, "We aren't trying to get rid of you. Your bedroom gets a stronger wifi signal that I need for work. We'd planned on getting the guest room fixed up nice for you. This visit is unexpected."

I shrugged it off, understanding the tone of her voice meant she wanted to understand my unforeseen visit at two a.m. "I'm really tired, Mom."

"Of course. You can tell us your troubles in the morning," she stated, confirming her curiosity and expectation of a reason for being there.

Her arm still draped over my shoulder, we walked into the living room. I sat on the couch and pulled my shoes off as my mom rushed to the hall closet and brought back a pillow and blanket.

As soon as my head hit the pillow, the night's adventures melted away into a dreamless sleep.

The strong odor of coffee and close chattering voices woke me. Popping an eye open I was alone in the room, but the house was small. Around the corner from the foyer was the kitchen. I imagined my parents talking over Sunday morning coffee as my mom scrolled social media on her phone and my dad opened the newspaper.

Once I was fully awake I joined them in the kitchen. Their eyes darted towards me with expectation. Ignoring them, I grabbed a glass from the cabinet, filled it with ice, poured coffee over the ice and stirred.

"Cold coffee, is that what we're paying college tuition for?" my father asked in a joking tone to break the ice.

I scooted out a chair and sat, taking a long savory sip of my makeshift iced coffee. It wasn't the double shots my taste buds had grown used to but, in a pinch, it worked. I met their gazes. "I was doing research close by for my paranormal studies class and lost track of time. Spirits are more active at night."

My father twisted his full lips. They'd never understood why I added the minor to my studies, however I still felt the need to try and explain how it worked with geology without giving away the truth.

"Ghosts leave traces on the earth; objects, graves, buildings, Croatoan carved in a gate post." I took another sip of my coffee.

Soul Catcher Episode 1

"Understanding the dead helps me understand the secrets of the Earth."

My mother smiled and reached a hand across the table towards me. "Whatever you think."

My dad laid the newspaper in his lap. "Sounds more like archeology."

Changing the subject, as we'd had this conversation in the past: "I have class tomorrow. Thanks for letting me crash."

Mom's brows furrowed. "We don't get much time with you these days, why don't you stay for dinner and we'll drive you home. We'll do an early dinner."

My parents' house was a mere hour and a half from the brownstone. I really needed to get back, but felt the stab of guilt for dropping in and leaving so soon, so I agreed.

The sun set early and the lights mesmerized me as we drove back to the city. Inside the city, they didn't seem so bright or captivating as they did driving in. I gave both my parents a kiss as my dad stopped the car, the engine still idling. Once I'd closed the door behind me, giving them one last glance and a wave, my father drove off.

Inside, I dropped my bag on floor by the door and flipped the deadbolt. An eerie feeling swept over me as my mind crawled back to the previous night. At my parents' the happenings vanished, now I faced them in the dark of my apartment. I flipped the lamp on and studied the room.

Goosebumps climbed my arms as Mike at the bottom of the stairs was a steady image in my mind. There weren't too many hidey holes in the small studio. Either way, it seemed I wasn't alone. Sliding the pickaxe out of my bag, I stepped towards the kitchen. Across from the kitchen was my bed, hidden by a bamboo screen.

Passing the bathroom, the door was wide open and the shower curtain pulled back. The room was empty. I stepped quietly over the floor, reaching the bar that separated the kitchen from the living space and lifted onto my tiptoes. The other side was empty.

I lifted the pick and caught it around the bamboo screen then pulled back quickly. It was empty. Sighing, I dropped onto my bed and took a deep breath. I jumped out of my skin and off the bed when my phone rang.

7

I pulled the phone out of my pocket. My mom's face filled the screen. "Hi, Mom."

"I want you to know how much your dad and I enjoyed the day. We love you." Her tender voice was almost apologetic. Knowing my mom, it was an apology for taking over my room. I was a grown woman now. Sure, it was nice to think about going home and sleeping in my comfy bed with all my stuff, trophies, and memories around me but it was time to start finding my own way and building my life. "I love you, too."

Soul Catcher Episode 1

The eerie feeling nearly vanished with the sound of my mom's voice, but not completely as I drifted off to sleep.

Nightmares plagued my dreams as the fiery-eyed dark spirit swallowed me. Trapped inside, I couldn't get free of the darkness. Sweat dripped from my forehead and tears rolled over my cheeks as my eyes popped open. I caught my breath and slowly my heartbeat returned to normal as I stared at the bamboo screen between my bed and the rest of the apartment.

I was safe. It was only a dream caused by my guilt. I splashed water over my eyes and stared at my face in the mirror. My hair was a mess, my eyes swollen, and I slept so hard I loosened my nose ring. Fiery eyes appeared behind me. I spun around but nothing was there. It was my crazy imagination, wasn't it?

If I set up the rocks, anything that entered my apartment would be drawn into them. I was being paranoid but the unnerving sensation existed if real or imagined. There were two kinds of spirits. Those that repeated the day they died and those drawn to the elevators. Only in the movies did they haunt people on purpose. The dark spirit of most likely Mr. Vickery hadn't been looking at me but beyond me. *Was he repeating the night of his death?*

I couldn't answer my own question but he was different than any other spirit I'd harvested and strong enough to get away.

The hum and splash of the espresso machine, combined with the rich aroma of coffee beans and the chatter of people, I sipped my double shot iced coffee and searched the computer. I had to know what happened to Mike. Blake had one paper and it printed every Tuesday. Great.

Luckily, the sheriff had a social media page. Ghost hunter Mike Medallion falls down the stairs at Vickery House. He suffered multiple contusions and broken bones and was rushed to the hospital where he remains in a coma. My shoulders dropped as the tension fell away. He was alive.

"Do you mind?"

I glanced into the dark eyes of Sharae. A latte with whipped cream in her hand. "Sure." I lowered the screen on the laptop.

"Why paranormal?" she asked as she slid into the seat across from me. Her dark hair tied up, displaying her elegant neck.

"I guess I want to understand spirits better." Really, that wasn't it. I got good info on haunted places and would have the credentials when graduating college to run a business of the dead. House cleansing, possibly.

She slid her pointer finger across the top of the whipped cream and brought it to her mouth, sucking the cream off her finger. It was a simple, innocent gesture that she probably did unconsciously, but it was suggestive. My pulse raced as I couldn't take my eyes off her full lips. Her mouth moving, I didn't catch the words.

"Tania," she waved a hand in front of my face, bringing me out of the moment.

"You want to go for a walk?"

She chuckled, "I was thinking the same thing. There's an art walk just a few blocks away."

Not a cloud in the sky, the air dry and warm. It was a perfect spring day, even though it was only February.

"What about you?" I asked, taking the attention off me.

"School, uh…" she chuckled again, "for me, paranormal is something I've always been interested in. I used to think I could see ghosts. I know, it's silly."

Not at all. If only she knew they did exist and most of what people understood, or thought they understood, wasn't correct. "No. I'm interested too." My reasons were very different than hers. "Are you going to be like a ghost P.I.?"

"Nothing like that. Look at that," she said, pausing in front of a painting of a woman in a hat. It was stylish. The hat tipped, shadowing one side of her face.

The afternoon was getting better with each moment. Sharae was classy, sweet, yet curious and mysterious. Her hand brushed against mine and she met my gaze as she turned her head slightly, then Metford spoke into my head and the moment vanished.

I'm busy.

We need to talk.

Not right now. Was being a harvester so intrusive a girl couldn't enjoy the growing attraction between her and another?

The comicay on my arm lit up green. I touched it and Metford's holoimage appeared. He could see me, and I him, but no one else could see him. He was at home. The smooth rock wall behind him gave that away. *I'm busy.*

Your date is over. We need to talk. His voice unusually forceful. He knew. Things were just getting good between me and Sharae. I caught her hand in mine and she stopped walking, her eyes studying my face.

"I almost forgot. I have a paper due for my earth history class. Can we try this again later in the week?" I made up an excuse.

She pressed a finger to her mouth. "I'm doing a haunted tour of the Lark theatre Wednesday night. I have an extra ticket."

"I'd like that."

She dropped her finger from her lips, stepped closer and pressed her lips against mine in a gentle kiss. That would have been a good place to leave it but I didn't want to. If I was going to get a Metford lecture about my careless actions then I wanted something to carry me through it. I pressed my hand against the small of her back and returned the kiss. Her lips parted, welcoming my tongue and curling my toes.

"I'll see you Wednesday," she said as we parted.

Soul Catcher Episode 1

That was a long time in coming. She'd been flirting with me for months and I pushed her away, not for lack of interest but for someone else. My lips curled in a smile, glad I'd finally given her a chance and happy she was so persistent.

I'd nearly forgotten all about Metford as his voice came into my head again.

There's another job for you, tonight.

I wasn't in trouble? Mike hadn't died, they wouldn't know! I hadn't thought of that, instantly assumed I was in trouble. He spilled the details while I barely paid attention, Sharae's lips on my mind.

Are you listening?

Yeah, of course. No, I hadn't been. *Where is it at again?*

He didn't hide the frustration in his voice as he repeated the details. By the time I reached my apartment he'd filled me in. Two men in their early twenties, one stabbed, the other shot. Both died in the alley. I thought to ask if he'd heard of any upcoming harvests, hoping to get info on whether Mike would survive, but decided against it. What he didn't know was best to keep unknown.

Soul Catcher Episode 1

I stepped into the apartment to grab my gear and instantly felt something was off. Worse, sharper than the previous night. The hair on my arms stood on end. Closing the door, I did a quick scan. Nothing was off, everything was in place, yet I couldn't shake the creepy sensation twisting in my gut.

The bag with my gear lay on the couch where I'd tossed it before going to bed. The creepy feeling was probably the close call from the night before. I tossed the bag over my shoulder and walked quickly to the nearest elevator. The unnerving feeling stayed with me as I jumped at every sound. That wasn't like me. I was a risk-taker, an adrenaline junkie who spent time exploring hidden worlds in caves and here I was freaking out at the breeze rustling branches.

Relief washed over me as I spotted Metford. He was a spirit and couldn't do anything if I was in trouble but he was a familiar face.

The alley was empty except for a dumpster behind the restaurant. Chinese, by the smell. It made my stomach growl as I realized I hadn't eaten anything except a muffin at the coffee shop.

Soul Catcher Episode 1

I placed the rocks in their familiar pattern, using the dumpster to block the view of anyone who walked by on the street, and waited as the spirits moved into the alley like clockwork. Spirits didn't change their routines at all. The men argued. I couldn't tell what about since I wasn't much of a lip reader and ghosts didn't speak out loud except the spirit of Mr. Vickery or whoever the dark soul at Vickery House was.

The screech pierced my ears and brain, almost rendering me helpless. Sharp phantom pains prickled my head at the memory. I refocused on the two men as they moved closer to the stones. One pulled out a knife.

A woman in a red jacket entered the alley. I tucked my head down and pulled out my phone, pretending to text. I needed her to hurry up and hoped she didn't kick the rocks out of place. She walked right through the spirits and purposely drew her eyes away from me as she stuffed a key into a door and entered the back of one of the stores.

The stones still in place as she'd skirted them without coming close enough to move any. The spirits stepped closer. The one with the knife threatening the other who put his

48

hands up in surrender then he dropped, phantom blood puddled on the cement beneath him. A man walked into the alley with a gun, talked with the other for a moment then twisted the knife from his hand, stabbed him and placed the knife in the stabbed man's hand. He placed the gun in the other man's hand, pulled his black gloves off and stuffed them in the side pocket of his coat then vanished.

The first man's spirit stretched as it was pulled into the middle of the rocks. The other man crawled along the ground, inching closer to the rocks until his body also stretched and was pulled into the middle of the rocks. Their spirits coalescing into black balls.

I could really take a couple pure souls right now. Holding the handle of the pickaxe, I aimed it into the center of the rocks and pushed the pick through one of the black balls and pushed it into the air. It wasn't stubborn and didn't fight as it pulled off the pick and into the Otherworld, vanishing from my sight.

One down and one to go. I collected the other and was ready to raise the pickaxe when the black blob expanded. "Metford, what's happening?"

Soul Catcher Episode 1

The black blob distorted and shot towards me, fiery eyes glowing as it attempted to break the barrier of the rocks, hitting and thrashing as it had last night. I ducked as a reflex but it bounced off the barrier. It was trapped. It screeched as a spirit pulled away from it – Mike. "Help me!" I dropped the pickaxe in surprise as his spirit was sucked back into the blob.

I grabbed the handle resting between the rocks and brought it up again. The blob expanded into warped shapes as arms and feet pushed out only to get sucked back in.

Metford stood beside me, studying the spectacle.

"What do I do?" I pleaded.

"What did you do?" he responded.

We didn't have time for this right now. "Don't follow up a question with a question. It's heavy!"

"You do what you always do, hold it up."

Both hands gripped tightly around the handle, I moved my feet further apart for a better stance and accidentally kicked a rock. It scattered into the middle. *No!* The fiery-eyed spirit flew past me as I scrambled to get the rock in place. The other blobs moved closer to the opening as I got the rock in place just in time to prevent their escape. I caught them with the pick and thrust them into the air. One shrank and vanished, the other bubbled and ascended.

I dropped the pickaxe and crumpled.

8

The one that shrank and vanished went back into the body of the living host it belonged to – Mike. That gave me some peace but I also had to explain how it happened in the first place.

Metford tugged at his beard as he listened, holding in any lecture he may be tempted to give. His face contorted in disappointment and thought. The malicious one had gotten away.

He didn't bother reminding me I should have told him last night or, better, should have brought him along, instead he explained how malicious spirits feed on fear and frustration.

"If we replay the steps of the other night your pick drew blood. Did you clean that blood?"

Oops! "No."

"That mistake aside, blood is a strong attractor. When you were distracted last night, you let down your guard and he used it to slip into the other man's body through the dried blood, but he can't take his soul unless the man gives it or dies. When you harvested those souls tonight the blood on the sickle drew him back. It drew both souls as they were battling. You kicked the rock out of place weakening the barrier and setting him free. We have to get him."

"How do we do that?"

"We lure him in with more blood."

Fantastic. No problem. I'd visit him in the hospital on his possible death bed, surrounded by family and take a vial or two.

No! I didn't need to. I had his blood still on the washcloth from the hotel. I reached into my harvesting kit and withdrew the rolled, bloody washcloth. "Will this work?"

Soul Catcher Episode 1

"Perfect."

"Are you sure this will work?" I asked as we set up the trap.

"We're in uncharted territory with you. The last harvester hybrid was centuries ago, but yes, this should work. The malicious spirit may be free but it desires to live in a body again and it's attracted to the blood. It's vested and probably weakened the man's soul. It will want to finish what it started."

The stones were set. I pulled the blanket under my chin.

"You have to stay focused. When you get distracted you weaken and make mistakes but you are stronger than him." Metford's words were meant as encouragement but reminded me of my humanity. A drawback for a harvester.

Hours passed before a cold breeze swept around me, dropping the temp in the room enough degrees to be noticeable. I pulled the blanket tighter over my shoulders.

A dark shadow moved from the corner, its fiery eyes burning into me. I pushed the last rock into place with my foot. The bloody washcloth beneath the couch I sat on. The pickaxe in my hand.

Soul Catcher Episode 1

Its dark form hovered over the rocks as they lit up, trapping it in the middle. It fought and thrashed and screeched as it tried to free itself from its prison. Coming at me. I didn't flinch but stayed strong and focused, taking Metford's advice. My ears ringing in pain.

It rammed the barrier created by the rocks. I tossed the blanket aside, stood. Pickaxe in hand, I stared into its fiery eyes. It molded to the side of the barrier then shrank away as I thrust the sickle into the middle of the spirit. I didn't wait for it to coalesce. It wrapped around it, tugged and tried to pull away. I thrust the axe upwards with both hands.

Its globular shape lifted from the pick, part of it wrapped around it. I stayed focused and didn't let frustration get the best of me. It shrieked but I kept my stance and hand steady as the stabbing pain ripped into my head.

The last of it lifted from the pick and it coalesced into a black ball before vanishing into the Otherworld.

Metford's straight lips curved into a smile. "Nice job."

I lowered the pickaxe and rested it against the couch, then lifted my hand for a high five.

I dropped backwards onto the couch. I did it! Now it was time to discuss something else. "I think we need some boundaries."

"Boundaries. Maybe we can work something out."

9

I'd battled my first truly malicious spirit and won but the victory wasn't really mine until I learned more.

Metford was right, we were in uncharted territory. I was a harvester hybrid only beginning to understand the art of harvesting souls and my capabilities.

I returned to Vickery House. The malicious spirit had been trapped in that room, whether on purpose or by guilt, I wouldn't know. There wasn't even a feeble salt barrier locking him in. Salt really didn't work as well as people thought. It was more of a misnomer.

Soul Catcher Episode 1

He'd also seen me. I was convinced of that based on his behavior in the barrier created by the rocks. As a ghost, he followed a pattern which had more power over him than whatever his intentions towards me. He was also focused on something beyond me.

Ghosts couldn't hurt people or interact in the human dimension, that's why he walked right through me in search of whatever was behind me.

It had been about ten when Mike and his son William had arrived at Vickery House that night. It was ten now. I leaned against the wall on the second floor between the testosterone room and the others.

At 10:33, two small children ran past me. They looked like brother and sister with their wild blonde locks bouncing on the top of their heads. They stopped and hid in the second room at the end of the hall.

The walls melted away into framing as they cowered, heads staring at something that I couldn't see because I'd sent him back to the Otherworld – the malicious spirit.

I squeezed the harvester rock. It gave me the ability to see the phantom images of those in the Otherworld.

58

Soul Catcher Episode 1

A stout man in his thirties walked towards the children. His hair long and wavy, trimmed that way on purpose. It was trimmed around the ear and long sideburns ran at least a half an inch lower than his earlobes. The fire in his light eyes burned inside him as he entered the room.

I'd done my research before returning. I was looking at Samual Vickery. The unwed, childless man that first owned Vickery House. He was a wealthy man and lived a lonely existence. Since he had no heirs, his money and house went to the town of Blake.

The children cowered, their arms wrapped around each other. The man yelled at them as he moved closer. The boy grabbed his sister's hand and ran to the other corner of the room, then through the framing into the hallway.

The man having a longer stride turned on his heels, followed them into the hallway and the little girl fell. No railing was in place yet. The boy grabbed her hand as she dangled over the edge.

Vickery could have leaned down and helped her up. Instead, he stood there and watched. I walked down the stairs and set up my rocks as the boy, unable to hold on to his sister, went plummeting with her to their deaths.

I wasn't going to let the children be tormented in death one more night. I grabbed my pickaxe out of the bag. Its wooden handle, made of elfin wood, firm in my hand. The pick and head made by trolls from metals in their lands and the gem in the eye of it a nycurium stone only found in Thraves. It connected with the six-sided star made by the rocks. It glowed a bright yellow as I lifted it towards the children's innocent souls.

Their spirits pulled into the middle of the rocks and coalesced into glowing white balls.

It was time to end their nightmare and send them to Tranquility. One at a time, their spirits freely left the tip of the pick and vanished.

10

As for Mike, after his spirit returned to his body, he woke from the coma and physically recovered. Mentally, I didn't think he ever would. Finding that ghosts were real might have been too much for him or maybe it was seeing me with a pickaxe raised high into the air. Based on his social media, he took an early retirement. His son started a podcast interviewing people who claimed to have paranormal encounters.

It seems William became a believer after the event but, who knows, maybe like his dad he was a grifter.

Soul Catcher Episode 1

Lark Theatre was built in 1930. It was the embodiment of wealth at the time. Its grotesquely elaborate gold trim, multileveled opera boxes on either side of the stage, and rounded dome ceiling and chandelier the size of my entire apartment hung from the exact center. Its light refracted off the many dangling crystals.

Aside from the ghost tours it was still in use and fully operable. In 1941 it burned, faulty wiring, and eleven people were killed, all staff. It was rebuilt in 1950 and since then there have been several sightings.

Sharae's lips curled into a smile as our eyes met. I set my boundaries with Metford. It was time to be a mostly normal college student again and have a social life.

Early in my training, I watched as harvesters captured the souls of the dying. Those on the precipice between the living and the dead. I clutched the harvester rock in my pocket and watched a world of spirits around us. What I did was different. I caught the souls of the dead, the ones who escaped, and sent them to the afterlife. I was more than a harvester, I was a soul catcher.

Soul Catcher Episode 1

I hope you enjoyed the story. Tania made her first appearance in In the Shadows - the first volume of the Realm Walker series. The Soul Catcher series will follow Tania in the human realm known as the Land of Lost Souls.

Keep reading for Tania's debut chapter from In the Shadows. Check out and read the rest of In the Shadows for the rest of Tania's adventure with Terra and discover exactly how she becomes a hybrid human harvester.

In the Shadows
REALM WALKER VOL. 1

5

A more compassionate and less witch-y side of Rosette was emerging. Terra was glad she could drop the 'aunt' bit, at least at home. She understood she had to keep it up in public or at the school.

Clyde ran in circles around her legs then balled himself and rolled across the floor dangerously close to her backpack. He scurried inside it and peeked his head and front paws out of the top. She understood his language and he was saying 'let's get out of here'. Sometimes he preferred the backpack over the harness. "Me too."

She'd completed most of her packing and was ready to inhale fresh air. With so many plants in the house, it would seem they'd have an excess of oxygen and it felt stuffy. She carefully lifted her backpack and pushed her arms through the straps. Clyde rested his head on her shoulders.

She glanced at her phone on the dresser. It still had some uses even if calls, texts, and her favorite social media were out of the question. The cell phone stuffed in the back pocket of her shorts, she grabbed her ear buds. Listening to downloaded music wasn't out of the question.

When she rounded the corner of her street onto the next, she'd spotted Kinzo, or rather his side braids and long ponytail. He'd walked her to the corner the other night but she hadn't seen which home he lived in. He and a girl sat on the porch of a two-toned house. The entire downstairs, including the porch and its thick columns and half the upstairs, a tan color. The upstairs on the other side a gray. It was almost like the house was divided in half and squished together, the front door being the center.

She wasn't sure whose house it was — his or hers. The girl with him was dark-haired and wore a long plait down her back. They were perched on a porch swing. Neither saw her, their faces glued to each other by the mouth.

Admittedly, she was a tad disappointed, but hopefully Provence Academy had other non-taken eye candy. She wasn't the serious type anyways nor was she gender picky. Hot was hot! To avoid being a third wheel, she cut across the street and plugged her ear buds in, hoping they wouldn't notice her, being so locked onto each other.

Her phone contained several playlists. She was cool with all kinds of music too. Today she felt like dance music. Clyde's face tickled her neck as he wanted to listen too. She turned it up. The warning on her phone said not to listen too loud, but for her there was no such thing.

When she reached the end of the road, past the strip mall she cut across, remembering the foothills past the forest. The air in Provence City was wetter than

Soul Catcher Episode 1

California, but not nearly as windy or chilly as San Francisco, although, it depended on the day. Some days were miserably hot and all she could do was lie on the couch beneath the vent.

Not really paying attention to where she was going or how far she walked, music blaring in her ears, memories of home filling her thoughts and Clyde riding her shoulder, she stopped when she couldn't go any further. Her foot meeting an invisible shield. Pain shot through her big toe as if she'd walked into a glass door.

She dropped the ear buds. On the other side of the barrier were hills. It was absent of plants and appeared depressed, desolate, and bleak. Higher up was a waterfall she imagined dropped into a river blocked from her vision by the hills. The falling water was odd and matched the color of the late evening crimson sky.

"Terra!"

Someone calling her name caught her attention. She turned to see Kinzo alone. Where was the girl he was sucking face with? He jogged towards her. She waited for him to catch up. Maybe he had answers.

Soul Catcher Episode 1

Clyde climbed over her shoulder and jumped. His little legs like spring loaded wheels, he caught up to Kinzo and walked with him. By the time Kinzo reached her he looked mildly winded like he'd run at least part of the way.

Unsure what to say, she sucked her top lip in then let it go. "I didn't want to interrupt."

"Nalysse is cool. You'll have to hang with us at school. There's a whole group. We could teach you everything about being elfin," he said, then touched her hair. The gentle brush of his hand sent tingles over her spine.

She rolled her eyes. "I hate it."

"It's cute. The first rule, though, is we wear our hair long. It's said to help improve our communication with plants."

Is that why the plants hadn't parted for her? She liked it short. Long hair irritated her. The whole thing made sense though. Rosette's hair was long too, even though she pinned it up in the horrible bat wings. The plant this afternoon twisted as if to listen in to their conversation. Maybe there was something to it. The girl he was sucking face with had long hair too. "Is that true?"

"I don't know. I've never cut my hair."

"Really?" She walked behind him and pressed her hand above his waist where his hair stopped. "That's how long it is. If you put it down, where does it reach?"

He touched his leg beneath his cute, rounded ass. He then suddenly changed the direction of the conversation. "You found the curtain."

Terra was easily side-tracked and had nearly forgotten about it, although the ache in her toe hadn't vanished. Her mind refocusing on it, she forgot to ask more about reaching her magic which was what she planned on asking him next. For now, it took a back seat. "What is it?"

"It's the barrier between Provence City and the realms. There are seven entrances but the only one you can move through is the one which you are from," he said, matter of fact, like it was common sense and everyone knew it.

She eyed Clyde scampering and rolling in the dirt. He'd need a bath. "So I can only go through the human…" her voice lingered, remembering they had a different name for them, "… commoner door. I'm also elf and dragon and something undefined," she said, remembering Rosette had mentioned her own mother found Terra's mom as an abandoned baby. They knew she was a hybrid and part elf, but no more.

He rested a hand on his chin. "I don't know. There are no hybrids. It's illegal and breaks one of the most revered covenants by all realms. I guess it could be possible."

Terra turned, catching another glimpse behind the curtain. Her curiosity at an all-time high. It was right there. What a cruel trick for her to see it but not enter. She pressed her hand against it as a child would against a glass window watching the rain. The curtain dissolved and her hand went through.

Kinzo stepped back, his eyes wide and glazed as if mesmerized. "That's impossible," he mumbled.

She glanced at him as he stared into the other realm. "Can you see it?"

He nodded. "Even a hybrid can't be Drakonian or vampire. They are walking dead and aren't able to…" Clyde scurried between them before Kinzo finished the sentence. He reached down for the little animal but it slipped his grasp. "No!"

Soul Catcher Episode 1

"Clyde," Terra screamed. Ready to save her little buddy, she lifted her leg to run and her hand was caught by Kinzo's before she stepped into the realm.

"No. Don't!"

She wriggled her hand free and crossed the plain in chase of the curious ferret who'd run up a hill and stopped. The rushing of rose-colored liquid from a series of waterfalls made it nearly impossible to hear anything else. Standing on his hind legs, his paws in the air, he froze. She caught up to him, collecting him in her arms. "I should have named you 'Mischievous'."

Glancing down, she saw what had captured his eye. A crimson red river. It wasn't a reflection of the sky or trick from the curtain. It was red! She was in Drakonia and that had to be Blood River. She hadn't taken Kinzo's words literally, that was her mistake, but if he couldn't enter the realm than he'd have never seen it.

Light flashed on the horizon, blinding her for a second. She blinked her eyes in response. When the spots disappeared, she noted what looked like tall buildings rising from the blood. The area was such a

71

wasteland, maybe it was only a mirage. A metallic odor accosted her nose, forcing dry heaves. City or not, her curiosity took a back seat to her gut's distaste for the river.

Clyde tight in her arms, she turned around and moved off the rocks. A true blood river wasn't her thing. She couldn't get through the curtain quick enough to Kinzo, who waited on the other side. Another couple steps and she'd join him. A piercing wail silenced the whooshing of the falls, forcing her to cringe, followed by a splash. She stopped in her tracks, gulped, and met Kinzo's pleading and dread-filled gaze.

6

Kinzo couldn't waltz across the curtain like she did. There was no time to concern herself with that now, someone may be injured. To keep her buddy safe, she thrust Clyde into Kinzo's arms and stripped the backpack off her shoulders, tossing it at him. "Watch him," she ordered and scrambled back over the rocks, forgetting about the morbid river.

Instinctively, she fought the gagging and dry heaves to reach the person crawling from the river of blood. The splash from the blood fall made the tan rocks red and slippery as she stumbled down them. The person reached the bank by the time she got there and rested on their back. She felt a bit of relief as it meant they were alive.

"Are you OK?" she nearly shouted over the whooshing of the blood fall.

The person stared wide-eyed, all but their golden-brown eyes covered in red. "I think so," she said. Her face pinching into a grimace as she licked her lips. "Yuck!" She spat, scrambling to her feet. "Is that blood?"

Terra didn't want to answer that question. "We need to get you somewhere you can wash off."

The person, a female by the sound of her voice and round curves, became defensive. "Who are you? Where am I? We didn't pay for this!"

"Don't snap at me! I came to save your life when I heard you scream and fall into the river from that bl… fall." Terra caught her words, not wanting to add more horror to the young woman's day and pointed a finger upward.

The girl's face distorted in confusion, blood dripping from her cheeks. "This isn't a gag or something?"

Soul Catcher Episode 1

"No. Tell me what happened. My friend," she pointed toward Kinzo, "and I will help you out." She crossed her fingers behind her back that Kinzo would help. He did say the elfin were more progressive than others, then she remembered Kinzo saying Drakonia was home to the vampires. Vampires drank blood. Did they prefer it fresh or from the river? Crap, she could be someone's meal gone wrong. "We need to move now, then you can tell us."

Terra's urge was to run over the rocks, but they were slippery with blood. Watching her footing, she stepped cautiously across the rocks. Her toe throb was a reminder of what happened when she wasn't careful.

"What kind of place is this? Are you sure this isn't a reality show?" the girl questioned as they made their way over the rocks.

Terra didn't have many answers for her. It was eerie to her too. "It's not a show." This was her new, unfortunate, life but it was looking better.

Once they reached the curtain, she breathed easier. The whole time messing in the realm she hadn't thought of the vampires occupying it and the dangers associated with that. Kinzo gawked at them in disbelief.

Terra put her hands out, palms up, elbows bent in front of her to say *what?*

His lips contorted, as if deep in thought with something to say, then he shook his head in dismay. "I know where there's a geyser. You can… you know," he said with a twirl of his finger.

They followed Kinzo to a freshwater geyser. Every few minutes, water erupted like a small fountain. Her name was Tania, she'd managed to tell them between gags and grumbling in disgust. She'd been spelunking with a group of friends when the cave sucked her down. It was her last memory before splashing into Blood River.

There was a lot to unpack, and she looked to Kinzo to do that, even though he seemed a bit confused and frazzled. It didn't surprise her he lacked any ideas and was more perplexed than she was. He hadn't gotten over how she was able to walk across the curtain when he couldn't.

"We have to help her," Terra said adamantly.

Soul Catcher Episode 1

"A young woman drops from a bloody waterfall in Drakonia, where neither of us should be, and you think we have to help her. What if it was her time and you entering Drakonia had a ripple effect on the harvesters, or maybe it was a horrible mistake, but we have her and they can't fix it?" He rocked on his heels.

What was he talking about? She discovered Drakonia not the harvester home, and what the heck was a harvester? So many questions. When someone was in trouble, helping was the right thing to do. "Harvesters as in harvesting souls or bodies? She's very much alive."

"Yes, Thraves runs alongside Drakonia. When it's someone's time, their soul is harvested and their blood is drained into Blood River." The words fought to come out as if he didn't want to say it.

Eww! That was disgusting and more than she needed to know. Now that she was away from the dreadful death smell and had survived to tell about it, she jested at him, "You get queasy."

He jabbed back, "I thought you were going to puke your guts up."

77

Soul Catcher Episode 1

They were both chuckling when a wet, but clean, Tania approached them. She looked like a shield maiden, with medium-length, dark hair shaved on one side and falling over her shoulder in waves on the other. Her skin a deep bronze with a blue studded silver ring in her nose and an armband tattoo on her upper right arm. The design was a snake eating its tail, or so it looked to Terra. Her golden-brown eyes studied them expectantly.

Rocked by her beauty, Terra lost her words. *Yeah, Kinzo was hot but Tania was smokin'.* It was Kinzo who broke the silence.

Tania listened, her face contorting various ways as she absorbed his words. Terra imagined she was as confused as she'd been, but didn't seem to harbor the anger Terra had. She'd also just lost her father. Her moods swung like a swing in a windstorm.

Tania's lips curled upwards. "This is too crazy for anyone to make up. I fell into a vampire river. That's so cool! It was gross, but who would imagine that vampires are real."

Not angry a bit. She was taking it very well. "We can help you get home," Terra suggested.

Soul Catcher Episode 1

"Why the heck do I want to do that?! I'm a thrill seeker and this place is way better than home." Emphasized with the momentary widening of her eyes.

Kinzo had some answers, at least temporary ones. She couldn't very well go home with either of them, or be seen in Provence City, but there was a cave where she could spend the night.

On the walk home, Kinzo grilled her about the curtain. Her opening and walking across it seemed to perplex him the most. His mind couldn't get past it, nor was he able to see the other side. What he saw was what he called a 'spinning, teal vortex' until she stepped over it, then the vortex vanished. The rocks and river became visible. But he couldn't take one step on the other side. The realm curtain, an unseen barrier, prevented him.

"I guess you need to be invited," she chuckled at her joke. Kinzo wasn't amused, by the serious expression on his face. "You know vampires have to be invited in so… never mind." His eyebrows smashed further as she attempted to explain her silly joke, eventually deciding it wasn't worth it.

What he saw or why he couldn't step to the other side was the least of her concerns. They had to help Tania get home and she clearly didn't want to, which made their job extra complicated.

"I have the magic touch," she quipped. "Plants are at your beck and call and for me the curtain dissolves and I can visit other realms. Maybe that's my magic."

"Impossible," he insisted.

They parted ways on the corner, not any closer to solving their little problem. The lights on in the house, Terra cringed as she opened the door, expecting *Lady Betty* Rosette to return. Instead, she was met with a forced hug.

"You took your comicay off. I didn't know where you were."

Comicay? Then she remembered the clear gel communication thing. "I took it off when I showered. I forgot to put it back on."

Rosette released her. "It's waterproof and indestructible."

That's what she thought. Terra had learned nothing was indestructible and if her father were there he'd laugh so hard his face would turn as red as his hair. She'd broken nearly every phone she'd ever owned. He tried the sturdiest covers and screen protectors. It was his mission to save at least one phone from an early death.

The one she had now was less than a month old and might actually last since it had limited use. "I'm sorry. I won't take it off anymore." Of course, she lied like any red-blooded teen. If that device could track her movements, she was glad she'd taken it off and, as a precaution, would take it off in the future.

Kinzo asked her to meet him at school tomorrow by the fountain. What had happened tonight needed to stay a secret between them.

Clyde, tuckered from the excitement, curled under the covers. He always slept by her feet then climbed up her body in the morning to give her wakeup kisses, as she called them.

Terra tossed her dirty clothes and reached into her drawer for PJs when a sharp pain like a stiletto carving into her chest erupted. She pushed her hand over her chest to lessen the agony and dropped to her knees. With each breath, her chest tightened.

Soul Catcher Episode 1